ferris wheel

Martha's
Baby Wipes

St.
MARTH

Karen Hughes's NECK

Bedspread Pattern
from our Motel

GEORGE & MARTHA

GEORGE & MARTHA

KAREN FINLEY

VERSO

London • New York

First published by Verso 2006
© Karen Finley 2006
All rights reserved

1 3 5 7 9 10 8 6 4 2

Verso
UK: 6 Meard Street, London W1F 0EG
USA: 180 Varick Street, New York NY 10014-4606
www.versobooks.com

Verso is the imprint of New Left Books

ISBN 1-84467-064-3

British Library Cataloguing in Publication Data
A catalogue record for this book is available from the British Library

Library of Congress Cataloging-in-Publication Data
A catalog record for this book is available from the Library of Congress

Printed in the United Sates by Quebecor World Fairfield
Cover drawing by Karen Finley
Cover and book design by Rex Ray

CONTENTS

BABY LOVE

"What a dump!"

I drop my retro paisley suitcase onto the shag carpeting and keep my arms up in the air, giving the hotel room a once-over. The room has a dirty window view of a neon sign that reads COLOR TV and AIR CONDITIONED. The king-size bed has a turquoise and aqua woven bedspread that must know semen as a spray starch. I try not to think about it. On the side of the room is a mirrored bar with a small fridge and a microwave. Above the bar is an iridescent cityscape of New York with the Twin Towers that looks like it glows in the dark.

"Oh, Martha. It's not that bad." George always insists everything is nice. He is such a goddamn Girl Scout at times.

"It smells." I whiff. "For God's sake, George, it smells like a wet dog."

George is whiffing in a serious mode, like a foxhound, and I have

to say he looks so endearing with his ears pointed up like a spaniel, I can't resist the temptation to rub him behind his mongrel ears.

What's up, dog?" George says without thinking.

Whenever George and I first get to a hotel we like to arrange our things. George gets the ice and opens up the items from the package store: beer, sparkling wine and snacks. I always bring my own sheets and extra pillows to make us feel at home. We listen to either standards, disco or whatever our mood dictates. I brought him a Jimmy Webb CD. George is humming to "Witchita Lineman."

"I am the lineman for the county..."

"George, do you want to put your show on the TV?"

George tries to tune in to the Republican Convention.

"Is that Maria Shriver sitting next to your dad?" I ask.

"Arnold's talking tonight." George answers and takes a swig of beer. He sounds jealous.

Sure enough there is Maria sitting next to George Senior.

"She looks anorexic," I observe.

"No, Martha. She was just born rich."

"Do you know who her father is? Sergeant Shriver created the Peace Corps. Her uncles… She's a Kennedy and now she is sitting with your father? What is she thinking? This is domestic abuse. This is sexual harassment, having to watch the high priestess of the democratic party sitting with George Bush Senior."

George is getting a little antsy. He always gets nervous when I bring up his family. I try to change the subject.

Martha doesn't drink from plastic

"Honey, pour me a drink."

While George is getting his beer and my sparkling wine I start to shimmy provocatively. George moves with me and brings the glass to my lips after we toast.

With one sip I jump back, feeling as if I'm going to pass out. I can barely catch my breath.

"Oh, George, this is awful."

"Martha, what's wrong?"

"George, you gave me a plastic glass!"

"Is that all, Mommy?" George says with impish glee.

"Mommy? Did you just call me Mommy?" I say, raising my voice but lowering the pitch.

"Mommy?" He responds softening his voice but raising it an octave.

"George, I am screaming out to my lover and you call me Mommy?"

Whenever I hear Mommy, I want to scream, yet I can't help being maternal. I wish I could love and be loved in another way.

Bedspread Pattern from our Motel

"Lighten up, Martha."

"Lighten up, Martha? Now, your negative mother complex becomes my problem?" I snap back.

"Martha, don't bring up my negative mother complex until noon."

George is behind the bar drinking his beer. I am holding my sparkling wine, becoming disheartened. Sometimes we're like an old married couple.

"You brought her up." I remind him thinking, I can't wait to get to prison.

"Maybe in your family you brought your mother up but not in my family," says George.

"Do you know whom you are talking to?" I try a different approach.

"My mommy?" George quips, getting my goat.

Oh, here comes baby. He always turns into Baby George whenever we squabble. Like a helpless infant, whose demands and frustrations need to be met now. It's been going on for so many years, it's hard to break the cycle of relating this way. Here it comes. The blood rushes up my spine and makes me stand straighter. I seethe into a paternal patrol mode, which excites yet frightens me. It is part of our erotic chemistry, irresistible to both of us. Like mother and son? Nothing new here. All I can do is to try and establish my own identity. And let nature take its course.

"May I remind you that you are speaking to one of the most influential women in the world today? Haven't you see my photo with Gorbachev, Clinton, Bill Gates and now, because of my impending imprisonment, Nelson Mandela? Haven't you read my books on appetizers, on brunch?"

"Honey, I hate to disappoint you but I'm not the kind of guy

who reads," George says and goes back to watching the convention with the sound muffled.

I take a standing position in the center of the room as if I am on trial, making a plea for the defense.

"When I was on 'The Charlie Rose Show,' Charlie asked me what was wrong with this country. I answered that we don't know how to grow a good tomato or stack wood. And Charlie listened to me."

George, glued to the set, says without looking up, "I'm listening, Martha. You know" he then adds, "even I would have done Charlie if I had the chance."

"I am important not because I fuck important," I point out.

George turns towards me. "I'm impor...porpor...impotent."
He sounds so goddamned fucking desperate. I have to work him over.

Why do I need to dominate George? Because I can. The only way

either of us is going to have any sexual satisfaction is for him to submit to my will and control. I didn't go to Barnard for nothing.

"You can't always get it up, George."
I know what's next. Oh, God, George is going to convince me.
"I need to see men in uniforms. I need to be on the brink of war," George declares. He takes a second as if language is too much for him. But he starts right up again. "Back in the day, when I was governor, I started my week with an execution."
He is slightly proud of himself and brings it back to me. He looks at me like he wants me. "You're kind of a gal in a uniform, Martha. You run your domestic affairs like the army."

I just can't resist him. He holds my waist.

George knows when to recognize me, compliment me, and I become his little girl. I melt for Daddy. I do everything for Daddy. I control him but he takes over. See, I do a good job and he appreciates me. He knows how hard I work. And everything I try and do. There

is something about the way he holds my waist like a corset, a too-tight belt holding in my locked desire. My constricted passion puts everything into its proper place and order.

"George, did you consider aromatherapy for the guards at Abu Ghraib?" I ask, slightly off the cuff.

"I don't like your crowd, Martha. Never have. If you get a slurp of spaghetti sauce on your napkin you feel like you just started a war."

I get back to unpacking my clothes. George is not going to upset my routine. "You did, George. You started a war."

"But that is not the point, Martha. I don't need to be reminded by your friends that I started a war. I know I started a war. I know I am responsible for killing innocent people."

"George, it always comes back to you. Do you care if I start screaming in the middle of the night?" I'm bringing up old wounds.

"I thought maybe you were playing with yourself in the bathroom." George is sarcastic.

Whenever I bring up our relationship, I end up feeling excluded. I panic that he is going to leave me, that I'm not a priority. Then I overreact,

It's plastic, George.

frustrated that I need him and want to be everything to him.

"Aren't you going to ask why I am upset? This is plastic, George. Don't you care why I am upset with the plastic glass? No, it's just another night seeing Martha. 'Oh, Martha, hey, it's George. Yeah, I'm in town for the Republican Convention. As soon as I can get away from Schwarzneggar and McCain, as soon as their lap dance is over, I'll be in your arms. Oh, Martha is screaming again.' Is that what you are thinking, George?" I was letting him get to me too much.

"I don't think, Martha."

George has a way of not taking me seriously. The room is getting too small for both of us. "I don't like this, George. It's plastic!"

"Yes, a petroleum product."

I'm trying to make a point with my raised plastic glass. I know sometimes I exhaust a point.

"This is my bad mood, George. It's a bad thing."

"I just put my face to the faucet or drink out of the carton, Martha. Don't make me responsible for the plastic glass. I am overextended as it is."

I don't know why I make so much of a small thing. But it isn't a small thing. The real issue is that I feel like a pit stop for George. The plastic glass is me, a throwaway. I am disposable.

"Then who's to blame, George?"

"My father. My father. My father. My father." George seems to have snapped. He throws himself on the bed spread-eagle, with his hand

Mr. President
I am ready to
be invaded and
hand over
the oil.

rubbing his thigh. "Now say goodnight, Martha, to your housekeeping Gestapo and give the president a blowjob before I invade another country."

George looks so cute getting all riled up. I instinctively become a sex kitten purring with a Martha Mae West come on. He slaps my bottom as I sit next to him and wrap my arms around his neck.

"When are you going to enter my country, Mr. President? I am

ready to be invaded and hand over the oil."

I place my body onto his lap with my breasts in his full view.

"Martha, I never get an erection from an uncluttered closet or from poached pears."

I become more playful and arch my back, bringing my heaving cupped breasts to his lips.

"You do too get an erection from my poached pears. Don't say such a ghastly thing," I say in my best Marilyn voice.

George reaches for the phone and places a call.

"Hello. May I speak to the concierge? Would you like to take Martha into the bathroom and fuck her for me? Yes, fuck her. She's all oiled up and ready to go. I am too important. I mean imporporpporposie importopuss... I mean impotent..."

I adore him as he hangs up. I love him when he fucks up.

"George, I don't know if I am witnessing attention deficit or domestic terrorism." I sit up and give instructions. "Your cock isn't going to fall off, George. I am not trying to castrate you. It is simple. Mommy doesn't drink from plastic." I say it with a twinkle.

George gets up from the bed and walks over to the suit he'll wear for his nomination speech. It is covered with a dry cleaning bag. He slowly removes the plastic and touches the bag provocatively. George is breathing deeply now and he starts to wrap himself in the plastic. I am a voyeur, watching George as he becomes aroused.

"When my mommy would have the dry cleaning delivered I would watch her as she removed her fancy dresses from the cleaning bags."

George is aroused. The plastic bag becomes a sheet of human skin. He tries to suffocate himself as he covers his face with the wrap.

"And the smell of the plastic... the sound, the shrill of the plastic... and the plastic... covering my mother, sticking to her body..."

George carries the sheer skin over to me and I greedily accept. He covers my body, my face. I run my hands over my sensitive areas until I am engorged. I am ready for him to do whatever he needs with me. I yearn to be his instrument of pleasure. His hand is on my tender throat with the plastic wrapping, taking my breath away.

"I love it when the dry cleaning bags arrive, you take your clothes off, cover your naked flesh with the silky see-through plastic. You glide over my naked torso with your pearls just barely caressing my chin. You glide yourself over me again. I want to touch so much. So much."

Then suddenly he is awakened and jump-cuts the fantasy, as if he was snapped out of hypnosis.

"Can't we just make this bipartisan and give the election back to me? Good night!"

I really don't know what the hell George is talking about but that isn't anything new. I'm going nuts. Sometimes George abandons our

passion so quickly that I understand the meaning of blue balls.

"George? George?" I try to appeal to him.

George grunts and acts annoyed as if I am disturbing him. "Ughhhhhhhhhhh."

I become like a bitch in heat. I try to fluff his cock but he stays flaccid. "GGGGGGEEOOORRRRGGGGE!!!!"

George just continues to grunt. "EHHHHHHHH."

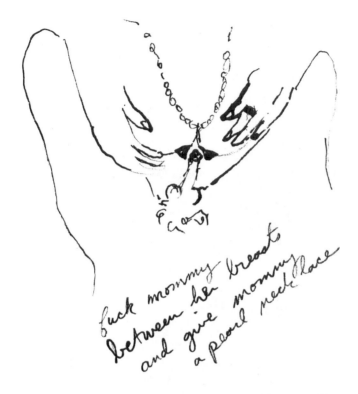

fuck mommy breasts
between her mommy flace
and give a pearl neck

I give it the good old college try and position myself on my knees. I squat down with my ample breasts squeezing his penis with the force of my cleavage into a bosom headlock.

"Fuck mommy between her breasts and give mommy a pearl necklace," I say while I pull at his tree. I'm turned on and wet. I repeat myself, but finally give up, exasperated. I sit up and demand, "You're the president. Do something!" I am such a bitch.

George goes to the phone again, dials and speaks, "Get me Condoleezza."

I'm sorry to push him, but I'm so frustrated.

"George, for God's sake, you can't do a goddamn fucking thing.

Do something, you stupid piece of shit! Do something. Do something!"

"Calm down, Martha."

"Any reason to call Condoleezza. Can't be away from Condoleezza too long. You want her, don't you?" I hate myself for revealing my jealousy.

"Yes, I want her. I want her. I want her. Last week I almost called her Cundolingis!"

Something blows up inside me. Maybe it's rage. Maybe it's envy of Dr. Rice. Her position, her relationship with George.

"Isn't my CUNTOLeezZa good enough for you, George?" I'm out of control.

"You're too good for me, Martha." George says this tenderly, trying to placate me. And I'm buying into any excuse I can find in order not to feel neglected. "Am I, George? Am I?" I'm so pathetic.

"You're the alpha male in our relationship and it does have its therapeutic benefits. What I have with you …it's all play, it's all fun, it's all in a weekend. With Condi, well, there is a lot more going on … It's not about food and cleaning under the bed, Martha."

"Don't tell me what you have with Condi! I don't want to hear about what you have with Condi! I don't want to hear about your walks at Camp David. I don't want to hear about spending time with Condi. What it's like to ask for Condi's opinion. What Condi thinks. Does she care about you like I do?" I'm practically sobbing.

Then George gets close to me, and does what he always does to win me back.

"That's why you are my mommy. I love my mommy," he chants like a little boy.

"No one loves me for me." I feel so sorry for myself.

"I love you like I love my own mother," pleads George with a grin.

I'm hoping that George will come to his senses and really appreciate me. Especially now that I'm going to prison, I think maybe this once I can get some Martha Time. Instead I lash out. "You are loving that sheep dog Barbara, that she devil mother ship when you are making  love to me! I understand perfectly now. I am Barbara. You're fucking your mother," I growl.

All George can say is, "No one loves me for me either, Martha."

There is nowhere else to go. I know George is my only chance for love. I have to love him.

"Call me baby." I need George.

We hold each other in a tender embrace.

"Baby, my baby. I love my baby. I love my baby. My baby. Baby. Baby."

"Baby. I love my baby. My baby. My baby. Baby. Baby. Baby. Be my baby. Be my baby Baby. Baby. Baby. Baby. Baby. Baby." We echo each other's needs perfectly.

I have to love my baby. He is my baby. And I am his baby.

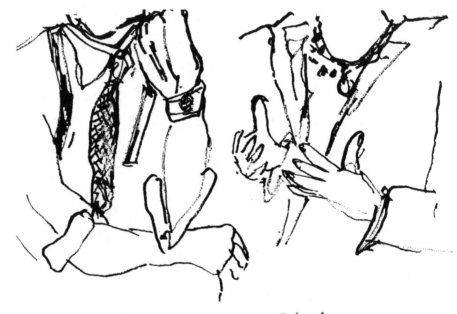

Larry King listens to Karen Hughes

WHAT'S LOVE GOT TO DO WITH IT?

Baggie of Powder Cocaine

"I don't understand why you wouldn't accept the deal from the Feds," George complains as he cuts lines of coke from behind the bar. He is always nonchalant about his recreational drug use. Now and then he snorts a line, then stares at Karen Hughes being interviewed by Larry King on the TV screen. I have better things to do.

I'm wearing my lemon-yellow and apricot-blush apron as I do a little room cleaning, sorting and fluffing up the pillows.

"Feds, meds, beds. George, I don't like their pillowcases."

"I don't understand, Martha, why you always have to play the victim. Do you want to go to prison? Is that it, Martha? I told you to pay the measly two hundred thousand dollar fine and you'd be free to do whatever the hell you want with potholders. Now look what you've done! Everyone is talking about Enron. Everyone is talking about Tyco. Every CEO is calling me and asking if this is all it takes to go to jail. A broker's call to cash in stocks on a tip? Isn't that what a broker is supposed to do?"

"I don't like their pillowcases." I want to change the subject.

"Maybe your people don't lie, Martha! There is something you didn't learn in Westport. Guilt and conscience are lower class phenomena. I lie. I lie all the time. We lie. It isn't about money anymore, Martha. It's about lying."

George snorts a line of cocaine and smiles. "Just like Bill, I don't inhale."

I don't like their pillowcases

I am torn between wanting to yell at him for getting high and ignoring his drug use. It is a constant battle for me. I move between withholding, making a scene, and hoping one day he will bottom out. But I know it's my problem. I can't do anything to make George stop. So, I act casual, disinterested. I suppose it's my way of enabling. But that's always a mistake. I tell myself that his problem will go away if I can keep the focus on me.

I take a deep breath and gather my strength. I say what I know to be true. "I'm not paying a fine, George. Martha doesn't pay fines for Martha is fine. Martha's opinion on everything has value. Martha's opinion and insight on everything from pillowcases to mustard to compost to geraniums has integrity and provides meaning in a meaningless, narcissistic culture of name brands in which the individual becomes lost. Now, excuse me, Mr. President, I don't know about you but I have a country to run."

I have to say that because I am equipped to lead, to make decisions. I lead a billion dollar corporation, and I started with nothing.

When I don't get a response I become disgusted, put on my glasses and examine the linen more closely.

"Do you know the thread count of this pillowcase, George? This isn't even a 200 count. I told you not to make the reservation with Hotel.com."

George slightly raises his voice and visibly mocks me. "Honey, why don't you just get married so we can have an affair like decent, hardworking Methodists?"

At that moment I'm exchanging the motel art for the floral Victorian etchings I brought.

"You are married, George."

"Can't I pretend?"

"It's true, George. You're a better liar than I." I give the etching an approving glance from across the room.

Coca leaves
and powder cocaine

George moves to the bed and brings the mirror off the wall to lay out the rest of his coke.

"Right about that, Martha. It's who I am. Let me tell you how it works. I had the Saudis funnel some spare change into my oil company Harken Oil then sold two thirds of my stocks and made $850,000…"

I have to interrupt. Sometimes George can be so self-serving.

"My father didn't teach me to lie like your father taught you."

"My father taught me that the problem with poor people getting rich is that they always feel so damn guilty and moral about making money. Martha, you just don't feel good enough about getting rich."

George stops to take another hit.

"You feel so unworthy of your success." He stops again for another toot.

"Like Martha deserves to be punished for making money." George takes another toot. "It's so unbecoming," George snorts.

"Acting so martyrlike," George sniffs again.

"So Catholic, Martha. Daddy might be an Episcopalian but he got this right. You have a persecution complex." With this he takes in the rest of the line of coke, pushes his head back and holds his nose.

St. Martha
patron saint of cooks & servants

single lay women

butlers, cooks, dieticians, domestic servants, homemakers, hotel-keepers, housemaids, housewives, laundry-workers, maids, sewers, travellers.

"You discussed our affair with your father?" I wasn't expecting to hear this. Did his parents have to be involved? I am horrified.

"Daddy told me the problem with Bill is that he picked too low in the heap. Gennifer with a G? Monica? Too damn young, and Jewish. Those people are always thinking when they are fucking. I don't think anytime, that's why I am such a fuck-up. HAHAHAHA. Fuck-up. FUCK-UP."

George is so goddamn pathetic when he is the only one laughing. I am not going to act like he is hurting me, so I don't respond. George tries to change his tone, but he can't control himself. He's high, pumped up, and won't consider me. So he stands up as if he is going to do something heroic. What's sad is that George can never say these things when he is straight.

"It's a good thing, Martha. I'm fine blaming my father. You want to blame my father? Let's blame my father. Let's get this taken care of once and for all and blame my father. We won't blame your father, Martha. *Let's blame my father.*"

George goes to the phone and places a call. I know I am in for a ride so I better get comfortable. I fetch my drink and settle on the bed with a couple of pillows. I am going to try my best to resist a pity party.

George gets on with the operator.
"Howdy, this is the president you didn't vote for. HAHAHAHA... It's a joke, Lady. . . Hey! Lighten up on the coop day tat and get George Senior on the line before I veto Medicare."
George mispronounces coup d'etat, which makes me cringe. I become embarrassed by George, in the same way I was embarrassed by my working class, Polish immigrant parents' speech.

"I know I didn't get the popular vote... Okay, let's lighten up on the coop day tat... Hi, Daddy. Do you know what a coop day tat is? Is that from rum ba ba bum a Christmas carol? ...Yes, Dad, I am that stupid. ...Yes, isn't it amazing that such a smart man like you could have such a stupid son like me? ...No, I haven't been drinking."

In spite, George takes a gulp of whiskey and places his hand on the mouthpiece and mocks a laugh.

"Daddy, do you know why I am such a lying son of a bitch? Because of you! That's right, Dad. I blame you for my fucked up life so now you can call your favorite son the Jebster and give him all the love I never received from you. He's the son who won the election for you. I know I couldn't win the election if it wasn't for the Jebster... Did I thank my brother? Dad, why don't you thank Jeb for me? You've done everything else for me.

"Don't compare your war with my war, how you did the war. I'll pay for it... Don't ask me how I am going to pay for it... Dad! Dad! Can't I do anything right? ...It's a war. People get killed. Wars aren't nice. You want nice? Nice? Nice talking to you."

George slams down the phone. The room is quiet. I can feel his pain. I offer the little comfort I can. He is so hurt. I want to make everything better for my baby.

"I was never good enough for my father either," I offer.

The phone starts ringing. It keeps ringing. George ignores it and so do I. Finally he runs in our cramped quarters like a hamster in its cage and places his hand with a firm grip decisively on the receiver. I rush over like Big Mama and put my hand over his and claw the phone away from his grasp. I dangle the phone off the hook, like a cat playing with a mouse,

holding the phone by the tail. I won't let him talk to that awful man. I hate his father. What a cruel bastard. Could he ever appreciate his son? I slam the phone down hard, hoping the banging would make his father shriek in pain like the pain he had caused George.

But George is like Jekyll and Hyde when it comes to his family, and now he decides to take it all out on me.

"You were never good enough? Do you know what it was like to have a father who was the head of the CIA? When I was circumcised my daddy had a listening device put in my foreskin."

I want to laugh but don't for George is banging his head in his hands and against the wall, in total distress.

"My father's voice never leaves my head!"

I try to approach and comfort George. "My father's voice is my voice. The constant criticism. The constant need for perfection. That damn fucking father voice penetrating me, invading me, entering me, tearing away at me. Yes, my father introduced me to sex at an early age—he mind fucked me." I hold George close to me.

George becomes more upset. He is shaking and sobbing. He is at the end of his rope.

"That's what this country voted for. A loser. A fucking loser who never met his father's worth. I am so tired of living out everyone else's fucked up relationship with their fathers. I want to live out my own."

George breaks down and starts to cry. I hold George close to me. I hold him and rock him in my arms.

I hush his tantrum. How can I tell George that his father is just an asshole? That his father is fucking with him? I want to protect him from the monsters under his bed, to slay his dragons for him.

"Why couldn't I have been there? Why didn't those planes kill me? Why am I here? All the people in the Pentagon, the World Trade Center... Do you think that my dad called once and said I am glad you are alive?"

George is like a baby, my little baby. All I want to do is rub his tummy. I want to give him all the love he never received. I want to be his everything.

 The phone starts to ring again. We stare at each other. We let the phone ring and ring and then I calmly answer it. The phone is dead. I look at George with bewilderment.

Then suddenly he turns on me. "Oh, Martha is disappointed. She couldn't speak to George Senior? Is this the way you fucked your daughter's boyfriend? Being nice and contradicdicdicdicdiccillatory... contracillatoy..."

"Conciliatory? Contradictory? Which is it, George? You really have no idea what you are saying."

"Could someone please explain to me why ideas are so important?" He says while giving me a Charles Manson stare.

I don't dare to respond. I am starting to get it. Now I am the enemy.

"Oh, you're so smart and wise, why don't you tell me how to grow a moon garden or burn sage to get rid of the Daddy cooties? You might as well fuck George Senior. Smarter, older, wiser George. And you both have something in common—you both want to fuck me over. You want to fuck with me, right Martha? Is that the game now, Martha? Let's

Sage

Sage Smudge Stick

get George? What's good for the goose is good for the gander?"

"What the fuck are you talking about?" I hate it when he gets paranoid.

Maybe he needs a combination cocktail. An antidepressant, an antipsychotic, and an antianxiety. I am glad I have my gardening.

"So I have to clarify myself to you now, Martha? It's a saying, Martha. What's good for the goose is good for the gander. A boring, unoriginal saying. For God's sake, Martha, you could never be with anyone average. But that's what I am, Martha. Average."

I clear my throat and sit down.

"Less than average."

I feel defeated. I am losing my libido.

George collapses on the king-size bed, spread-eagle.

35

"I am married to a librarian, Martha. I don't want to be fucking the Dewey Decimal system… Get George Average's attention, put on a thong, Martha, and enter my world of attention deficit!"

I don't like it when a man pits woman against woman, especially the most powerful man in the world. I don't want to be in competition with Laura. But I guess that is what George does, constantly compares us. Sometimes I imagine how George does or doesn't speak to Laura, or how he reacts when my name comes up. Laura is always the good-natured partner.

"George, I realize you don't understand me, but don't belittle me.

"While you are bombing Mesopotamia, I am thinking about pies. I am thinking about crusts and strawberry rhubarb. I am thinking about Lilies of the Valley. I am thinking about stuffing the goose. Have I hurt

anyone, George? Have my hydrangeas hurt anyone? Am I dangerous, George? All I am doing is thinking about my next segment for "Living." That's all, George. I know you have a country to run. You have a country to destroy and occupy. You have nations to overthrow, empires to assemble. I am taking the small bit of dignity that I have and trying to do the best I can with a coat of paint and index cards while you and your cast of psychopaths destroy the planet. Yet I am going to jail. I am guilty because I try to make this ugly world of corrupt, mean men a little more pleasant for people who don't have as much power as you."

"Honey, your next segment is in stripes. Hahahaha… Sorry, I couldn't help it… Hey, sweetheart, tell me a good Brussels sprout recipe for when you are in the can! Hahaha, honey, it's a joke…"

For a moment I have to laugh. I love the way he makes fun of me. But this is too important. I need him to listen to my politics. I can laugh at myself later.

"Look at you. You won by losing."

"Sometimes you win by losing." George pours another drink, glancing at Jeb on the TV.

"How does it feel, George, all this power, and no vision?" I'm not going to spare him this time.

"Do you know what it is like to have a job you aren't qualified for?" George whines.

I shake my head. I am ready to compare grade point averages. George goes for his stash and starts to roll a joint from behind the bar.

"That son of a bitch, Gore, he won. But does he want this goddamn fucking job? I don't think so. Did you see him at the prayer mass after September 11? He was all wooly and sweet, probably rolling a

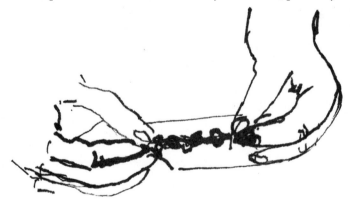

doobie, a fatty, on the way down."

George is licking the rolling paper and placing the joint around his lips, ready to light up.

Just then the phone rings. He is so cranked up, he overreacts to the phone ringing.

"They are trying to kill me! They have electric hydrothermal  nuclear energy right here in the wire. I can't answer the phone, Martha. I can make calls out but I can't answer."

This is crazy.
"It's probably your father calling back."
"It doesn't matter, Martha. They want me dead."

The phone keeps ringing. I know George is manic, delusional and paranoid. But this is more extreme than usual. The job is really getting to him.

"It's probably your father. Talk to him…" I try to get him to come to his senses.

"I'm not talking to him. He wants me dead, too. You have to tell him I can't come to the phone. The killing current is sent over the satellite into my DNA. Junior is not talking to Senior even if he apologizes."

Maybe it's wrong to intercede, but I have to take charge. I answered the phone and speak right away.

"Do you know what George wants to hear from you? 'I love you, George. I love you with all my heart, George.' It is time to tell George you love him."

I start to giggle when I realize my mistake. I hold the phone away from my mouth with my hand on the receiver and whisper to George, "Oh, honey It's the other president…"

"It's Dick? I can't touch the phone. You have to talk to him. He wants me dead, too. He's just like LBJ… I'm sitting in the convertible in

Dallas. Ah… it's Lee Harvey Cheney…"

I try to remain calm.

"Hello, Dick…"

George is standing in the middle of the room petrified.

"No, I don't think George can talk today. Bye."

We rush into each other's arms and embrace. In our tender moment, George and I understand and comfort each other. Sometimes the expectations are too much to fulfill. It is as if we live someone else's life, and someone else's idea of success. What we have both sacrificed is intimacy, our privacy. We both became our parent's ideal. But we are insecure and hide our unloved selves from the public at all costs.

George gets serious.

"We would never do this to our child. We would never name our

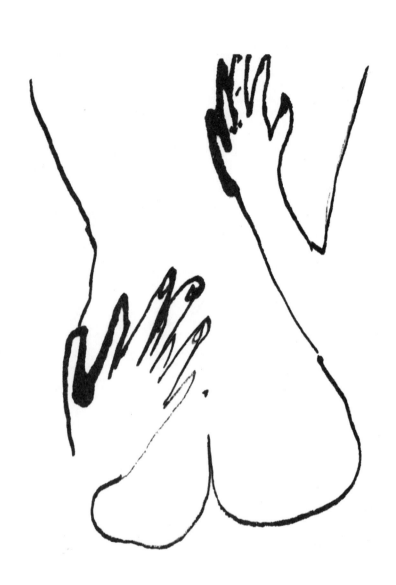

son my name."

George is holding me close.

"We would never name our son your name," I murmur.

"And we would love him for him and he could do whatever he wanted. He could manage a restaurant, or start a pizza parlor or do nothing..."

"George, did you know our son is the same age as you were when we met? He's 29."

"Tell me how it happened," whispers George with tenderness.

I share our intimate past.

"It was 1975 and I was in the Rye Hilton. You were visiting your family in Connecticut. I had a business, Martha's Baskets, and was making a delivery. You needed to get a way from your family, so you went to the bar at the Rye Hilton. I walked past you, carrying a Martha basket, and I tripped. Our eyes met and we fell instantly in love."

"I wanted you, Martha, from the very first moment."

"You were so simple, so easy going, so I stopped and had a wine with you, and another, and I couldn't drive... Remember?"

He holds me closer and tighter, I can hardly breathe.

"Some of it... That is why you need to tell me again."

"Well, then I got pregnant."

"...We wanted the baby"

"We knew we couldn't...and we should have...my life at Turkey Hill..."

"I didn't want to force you... I didn't think you could possibly love me. You were so perfect. And I was so..."

"But then I fell, I fell..." This is so painful for me to remember.

"I wish I could have been there..."

"Our boy would have been so perfect, like me," I add.

"I would love my son like I wanted to be loved…and he wouldn't look like me…and he wouldn't be like me… He would love his mother and his mother would love him back. You would love him…" says George.

I continue where George left off.

"I would love him like I love you. I love my baby, be my baby. My babe, my baby."

We hold each other and whisper and share our pain, our love, our loss.

"Be my baby…my baby, baby my baby, baby boy, baby boy, baby, baby, baby, baby…

"I love my baby."

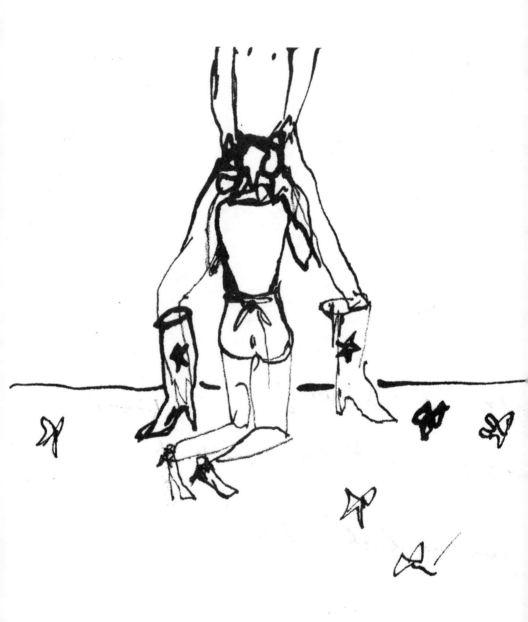

MAKE LOVE

"Did you ever fluck… fll… fuck Clinton?"

I was always told not to talk with my mouth full and my mouth was so full. I am on my knees with George standing on the bed while I gave him a blowjob. He has my head in his hands pulling my head taking everything he had to offer.

"Did you ever fuck Clinton?" George demanded again.

I was choking, gagging as I swallowed his cock.

"Did you ever fuck Bill? Did you ever fuck Bill? Did you ever fuck? Fuck fuck fuck… Jesus… Jesus. Fuck Jesus… Jesus. Fuck fuck fuck Jesus… Fuck."

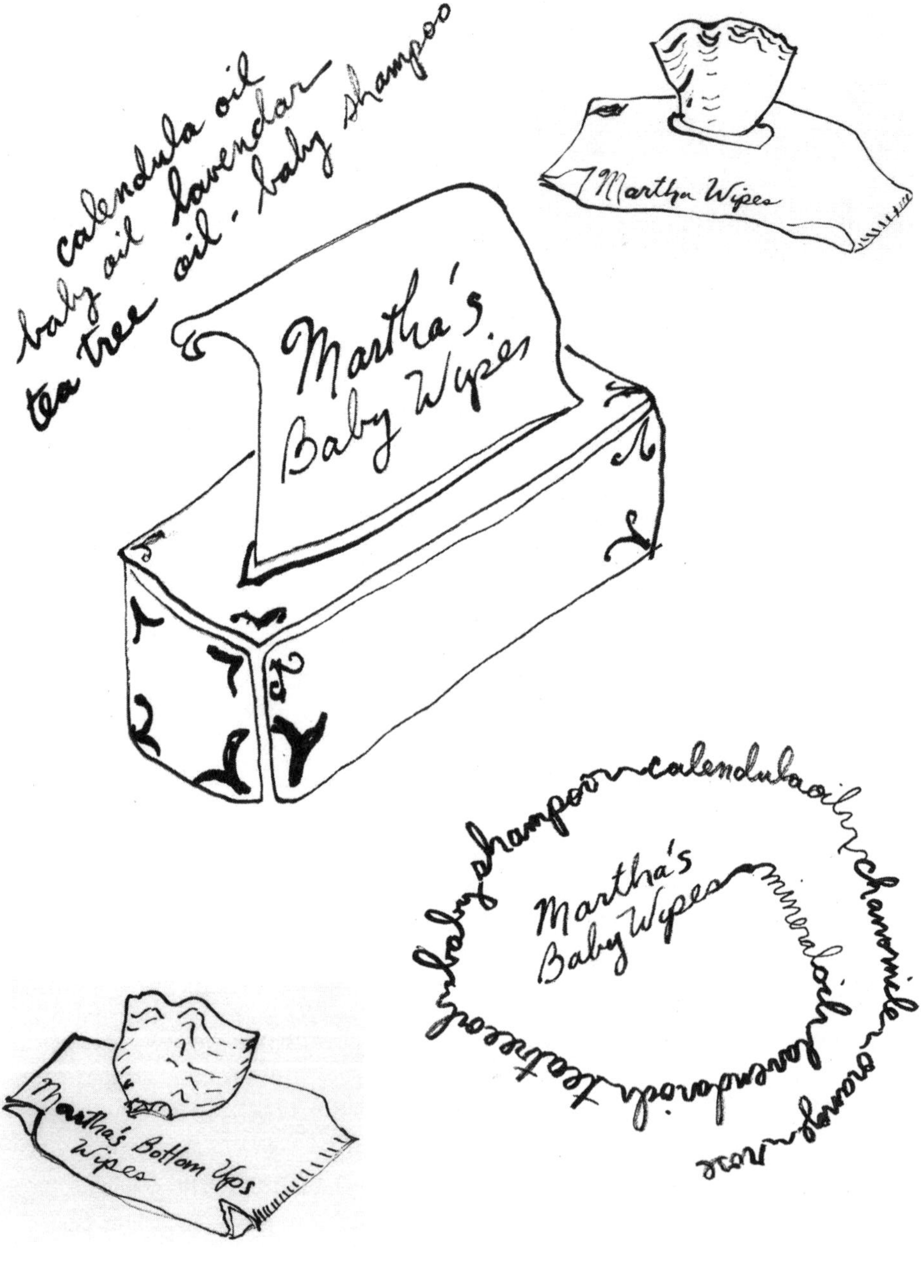

calendula oil
baby oil lavender
tea tree oil · baby shampoo

Martha Wipes

Martha's
Baby Wipes

Martha's
Baby Wipes

shampoo calendula oil chamomile
baby mineral oil avocado
oil tea tree oil lavender oil nose

Martha's Bottom Ups
Wipes

George likes to think of himself as a man of God. And as all men of the church, he orgasms with a final fuck Jesus fuck and collapses in the pew.

My mouth is full of his coconut smoothie and there is no way I am going to swallow his protein shake. His cream is drooling out of my mouth like a bungee cord.

I reach over and open up a new box of Baby Wipes. Why didn't I invent Wipes? Maybe I should consider creating a Martha Wipe. I make a mental note.

I stuff about five Baby Wipes in my mouth to soak up the wiener pus. I have to get the taste out of my mouth. I rinse my gums until all I have is baby powder taste. And as soon as Georgie smells baby his baby will become a biggeeee!!!

"George, I love you for your baby body and not your baby mind," I say as I wipe and clean his heinie.

I do get turned on by George becoming a baby boy. Sometimes I wonder why. I guess I like the feeling of dependency, his complete immersion into mama. I am propelled by my own complex. Sometimes I just don't want to think so much about what feels good for me. And that is what George gives me, guilt-free role playing.

playing dead

"Baby doesn't mind Martha."

George spreads his legs for me. He is naked except for his boots. If you didn't know he's kinky you'd think he was pretending to play dead like a doggie on his back in submission with all paws in the air waiting for his belly to be rubbed. That is my signal to gather my special treasure chest.

I open the mistress lock and remove a special rubber sheet for "baby" Georgie to lay on. Georgie is giving me baby coos.

"What a smelly baby. What climbed up the smelly baby and died? Oh, what a filthy, stinky baby." I am gagging.

"I'm a dirty baby. So dirty." Bushie is twisting his nipples.

"You are a very dirty baby. Someone has to clean the baby. I'm the one who has to clean the baby. There is no one else who can clean the baby."

"Clean the baby. Clean the baby," coos Bushie.

"I will clean the baby because I am the mommy. Mommy cleans the baby."

Part of our relationship is based on George needing to be infantalized. I'm his ideal mother. I never consider our ritual particularly

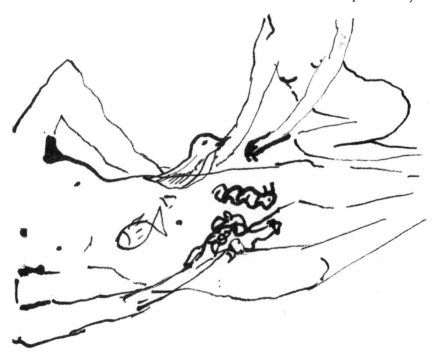

kinky, even while I'm shaving and diapering Baby Bush, because I know it's the underpinning of all relationships. It's all about Mommy. It always comes down to Mommy.

I place several stuffed animals on Bushie. A glowing angelfish. A small pink poodle. And a rainbow caterpillar. Bushie starts holding his dick and having it speak to the animals.

"'Martha, you make a better Hilary than Hilary.' That's what Bill would always say. 'Martha, you should really run the White House.' 'Martha, I love the way you care about Christmas decorations. If only Hilary cared about decorations the way you do, then the country would love her.'" I was recounting my pillow talk with Bill.

Mommy's a Ball Buster

"But you don't have a sense of humor either. And you are both ball busters."

George is prompting me. I'm getting aroused. Our game is in full swing. I turn on the electric shaver. I am holding George's balls so tight you can see the sperm being made.

"Mommy's a ball buster. Mommy's a ball buster." I grit my teeth and snarl as I speak.

I start shaving the nipper's pubes and anything scraggly. Mommy needs a clean baby. George is a squealing pig. I have wrangled his legs like roping a steer. I look like I'm branding my bull.

"Baby's afraid. Baby's afraid." Bushie pleads.

I push the electric shaver to my baby's face so his eyes are all bugged out.

"Listen up, motherfucker. I make a goddamn decent living as the dominating mother that you fear, loathe and despise."

My tone makes George wince. It is too real.

"Okay, Freud, don't be so goddamn fucking useful with your Oedipal theory. Keep it simple, Martha. You're the mean mom."

Baby wants more than discourse.

This might be me at my most terrifying, if you don't count when I was chopping cabbage standing next to Katie Couric.

chopping cabbage

"Mean Mom wants to be hated because she can't be loved, because she wants her father and knows she deserves to be the mother."

"I think that's my problem too." George always wants to fit in.

Mean Mom now takes out the toothpaste, the kind with white, red and light green stripes, a breath mint version of our flag. I squeeze the paste onto Baby Bushie's groin. I open several jars of patriotic glitter and I geld our president's balls with blue fairy dust so they become luscious sapphires. Or in simpler terms, blue balls. Next, I paint his now limp penis with a red glitter goop so he is gifted with a precious ruby to take the piss out of.

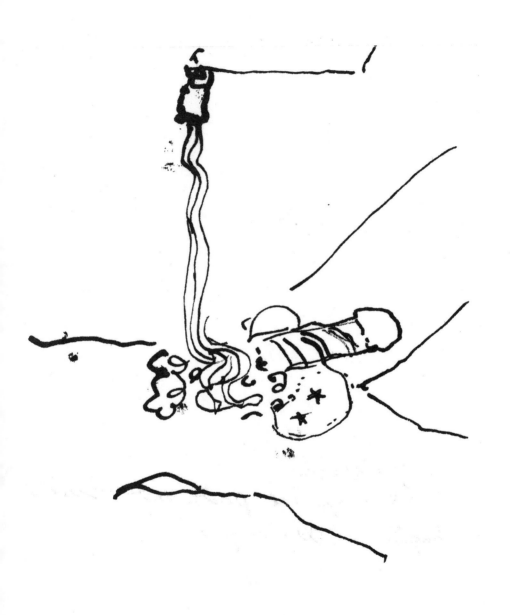

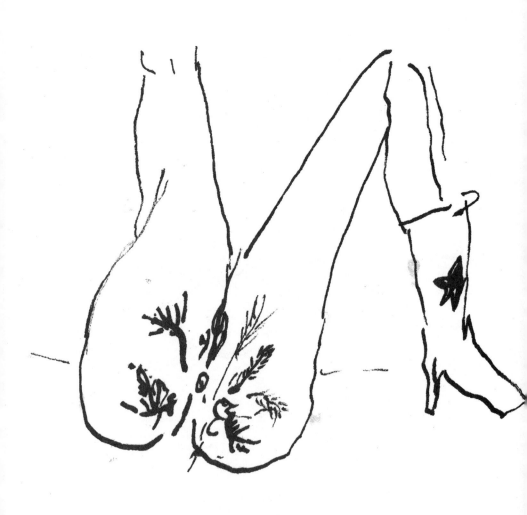

My body is electrified, charged while I take command and control Bushie's masculinity. I am penis. I am Commander-in-Chief. He is my baby. But I want to know all of Baby's dirty secrets. All of his hidden fantasies. Mommy wants to know.

"Did you ever walk in on your parents having sex?"

I proceed to take out an ornamental canister from Harrods that is filled with red, white and blue feathers. Carefully I place the feathers on the toothpaste glue in a cohesive exacting motion until I have completed a patriotic feather diaper with red, white and blue hues.

"From the time I can remember, I always feared my parents would kill me. I don't know why. All I know, Martha, is my parents wanted me dead, out of the way and gone. I stayed in my room for hours because I believed if I left the room they would hack me up in pieces and serve me to Jeb and Neil. I lived in terror and fear. Baby's afraid. Baby's afraid!!!" Bushie confesses.

I'm not interested in Georgie's persecution complex. I am thinking of sex.

"Did your parents ever watch you masturbate? Play with yourself?" I love the visual.

"Did Bill ever watch you and Hilary get it on?" Bushie asks. He is obsessed with Bill Clinton.

"That's what all the Republicans ask. I'm a twin. I am a better version of Hilary. But Hilary has no taste," I add.

"Her puss has no taste? I don't believe that, Martha, for one minute."

"Okay, she had Whitewater. I had Imclone. Blonde. Smart. Powerful. It's a class issue." I say.

"You might have class, but Hilary has ass."

He is starting to get on my nerves.

I think it might be time for a little spanking. I am holding George's legs with his ankles over my shoulders, slapping his bare ass.

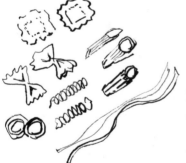

"Like a Botticelli." I'll show Bushie who has the class and the education and the better ass.

"Oh, like a booticelli. Is that like vermicelli? Fettucine, linguini, fusilli? They all sound pornographic. I am going to have to get the FCC to regulate cookbooks. That bootticelli pasta is making the baby hungry," Bushie says while patting his belly.

Bushie pats and pokes his tummy. He gets very baby aggressive; he has a tantrum. He needs to be fed. I love my baby but I know Baby needs to remember he is the baby and I am the mother.

I go into my treasure chest and find Georgie's bottle. I rush to the bar, unscrew the nipple, and fill the baby bottle with beer. The beer overflows like Niagara Falls onto the floor. I slowly walk up to the love of my life, that father of our country, take Baby in my arms and place the nipple to be suckled.

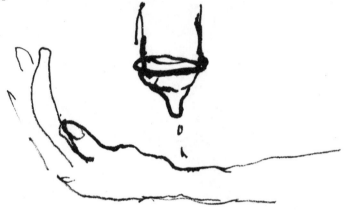

Baby Bushie sucks and I feel my breasts let down in sympathy.

"Does Bill have a crook in his crack uh uh uh a crock in his cake… in his cock?" Poor Bushie. He can't stop himself.

"Well, I don't know. He wouldn't fuck me. You know that, George."

"Wait a minute, Martha. I just asked you if you ever fucked the president?"

"You're the president, George."

"Oh, that's right Martha. I forgot."

LOVE & WAR

I know our time together is short-lived. So I relish our moments of quiet. George and I are sitting up in bed, in each other's arms. I am stroking his hands, his palms, interlacing my fingers into his. George loves to feel the soft spot behind my earlobe, the back of my wrist.

But I also need to think about my future.

Back of Wrist

"George, I need to redesign the world."

"Honey, can't we keep your work out of our love life? I just want to get a little high and watch 'The Sopranos.'"

"I can go big on this, George, but only with your help. It is more than infrastructure, George. We can redesign America with a Middle East accent. In the 50s, after Pearl Harbor, Hawaiian themes overtook

 home decor. Everyone was wearing muumuus, and throwing tiki parties. Now, with my connections at Kmart, everyone in the US can be pitching a tent and building their own mosque."

George chided me: "Sweetheart, I know we both are involved with domestic issues, but Kmart is not Iraq."

"Kmart isn't Iraq, but that doesn't mean Iraq can't be Kmart."

"Honey, I hate to disappoint you, but Cheney isn't making money in shower curtains."

Everyone has a kitchen

George never listens to me. I face him, hold his shoulders passionately and continue my plea.

"Everyone has a kitchen, George. Give me a chance. I want to redo the lifestyle in Iraq. This is more than religion, George. Once I introduce a culture to Shabby Chic and extra virgin olive oil, they'll pay lifetime dues to be in Martha's club. We are talking utensils. Utensils,

George. Utensils! Everyone needs a utensil. Everyone needs an herb garden!"

I get so excited, just thinking about the possibilities.

"Not an herb garden, Martha. We want them to buy things, not grow them. Cheney thinks it's all in fast food."

"Cheney? You are listening to that bald headed, uncouth fart machine on his sense of style? George, you are going to need me. America needs me. I can transform the horror of the panty headdress into dust ruffles. I can transform the hooded prison garb into the perfect black dress. I have the solution, George."

I should be running this goddamn country.

"Easy, Martha."

"Maybe Cheney's right, but why wait for him? I want to open McMohammed Kabob. It's a good thing!"

George looks at me perplexed.

"Look, George, Sony in Japan was started with American money. And if we are lucky, if we play our cards right, Mickey McJesus will be coming in a six-pack on the Gaza Strip."

Using the Jesus calling card always worked in drawing George into the conversation.

"You're right, Martha. These people need to liquor up so they can find our god our way. It's time these people learned to take the edge off with alcohol. That's the way I found Jesus. With alcohol. Drank myself to oblivion until I found the Lord."

"George, we don't want them to be shitting red white and blue. Only wiping their ass on the good old USA greenback."

"We could bring in McDonalds, Disney, throw in a theme

park and call it Mickey McMohammed. Make a movie, a cartoon on the Passion of Mohammed. Make Mohammed a mouse. The Moslems need a mouse. A Moslem mouse. A Mouslem. Make Mohammed a mouseketeer. Then we get the kids meals and toy franchises and everyone is happy."

George is on a roll and can't stop.

"And another thing," continues George.

"Make it a good thing!" I think I have him. It's a slam dunk. But all of a sudden George becomes hesitant. It's the cowardly George, indecisive, exasperated George. Here it comes. Here comes WASP culture. He is going to be concerned about what others think.

"I don't know, Martha. It might not look good."

"Might not look good? This is a new George. Since when have you been concerned about appearances?"

"I want to save the theme park for when I leave the White House."

"Oh, don't start now with priorities, George. You can never be spontaneous. Oh, go read a book with Laura and turn on the night light."

I am annoyed.

"Martha, I can never process anything with you."

"Okay, I'm listening." I cross my arms defensively.

"I plan…" starts George.

"Oh, George has a plan." I'm sarcastic. He is revising my vision, my fantasy.

"I plan to make a theme park based on all the presidents."

"All the presidents? Really, George? That is quite an undertaking." Now I'm cynical.

George does his best to ignore my cynicism while maintaining his vision.

"It will be a theme park based on all the presidents."

"You just said that dear. All the presidents. Don't need to repeat yourself." I am in kindergarten.

"It will be a theme park based on each and every presidency. And considering…" says George.

"Considering… Sounds very NPR. Sounds liberal, considering?"

"And considering…" George repeats.

"Are you really going to consider everything, George? Are you? Are you considerate, George? Really, George, you have never considered anything except the easy way out of anything."

I am raising my voice and ready to give him hell.

"Since there is always a new president…" says George.

"Never knew that, George. Thought we were in a dictatorship or monarchy under King George. Thanks for telling the subjects!"

 George and I always clash whenever we discuss the future. I know that I am not in his plans. And I realize how little emotional security I have.

George's face slowly becomes the color of Red Bull.

"Since there is always a new president, the theme park will continue to grow and grow. And I will make appearances. And my library will be there, too."

Yep, George is mad in the bullpen.

"Since you don't read, there will be plenty of open space for Frisbees."

I have to tell the truth, so help me God. The conversation is going nowhere with this idiot. I get up and put on my floor length negligee. I

catch my form in the closet mirror. I am hoping for a minute that maybe he will just stop thinking about all of these plans and look at me, be with me. I see my sillouette and I wonder if maybe I no longer please George. Men are so dependent on the visual. I wish I had gone on the Atkins Diet before seeing him. But during the stress of the trial I had to have my comfort food, and I puffed out. Maybe when I'm in prison I can skip the carbs and trim down.

George shoots up from the king's throne. He knows I am smarter than him and he hates me for it.

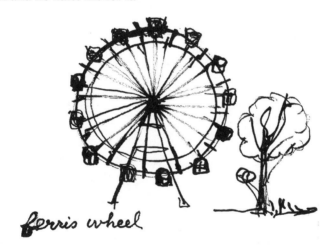

ferris wheel

"What do you want? A theme park for your people, the Pollacks? You're not a Stewart. Stuart is the surname of the queen of England. You're a Kostyra. Martha Kostyra. A Polish Catholic eating stuffed cabbage and wearing a babushka."

He follows me into the bathroom. I turn on the shower.

stuffed cabbage ingredients

head of cabbage
1 # ground beef
onion
egg
slice bread, or bread crumbs
mustard
parsley
pepper, salt
tomato sauce

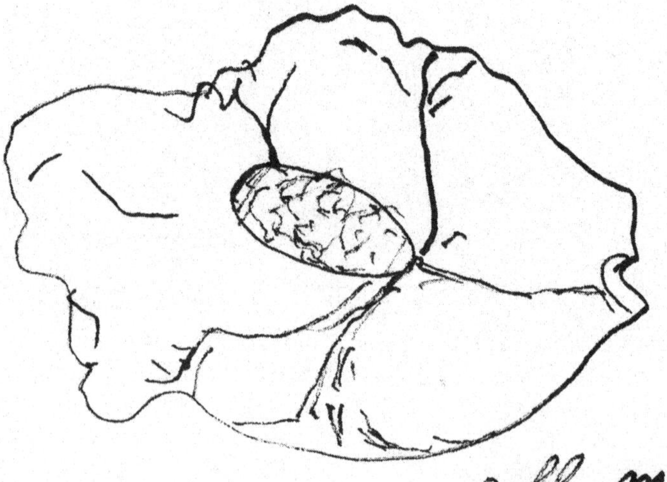

roll meat
mixture in
cabbage

"I admit it, George. I don't like who I am. But I am so tired that every opportunity you get you belittle my ethnic heritage," I say, waiting for the water to get hot. I take off my negligee and hand it to George to hang on the door while I step into the shower.

"You think you are the only one entitled to not like who you are, Martha? I don't like who I am. But I am not allowed to hate who I am because I have all the power. Is that it, Martha? You had to work for it. And we all have to pay now. Bitter, resentful Martha. Well, I hate my parents. I hate my life. I hate myself. I hate this country. I hate Martha, for being more of a man than I am."

I soap with the small bar of motel Ivory and a threadbare washcloth. Now George has started something he will regret.

"Oh, is that supposed to hurt me now, George? Put me in my hurt place? Let's start the game, George. Let's play motherfucker. I can't help it, George, that your mother Barbara was the real father of this country. That Barbara was the real George Washington of this country," I shout over the water pressure.

father of our country

"Don't start Martha…"
I peek out of the curtain and let the shower hit my back.
"Enough with your father. Let's see how your mother fucked you up. Your mother was the real man in the family. She even looks like George Washington. You thought your mother was a man, right George?

She is in drag, walking around with those fucking pearls. She married your father and gave birth to a president. She is probably the only woman to be fucked by two presidents besides me. You are a motherfucker, aren't you? A real motherfucker. Fucked your mother right in the birth canal."

I know I am going a little hard on George and his mother. But probably it is because he never finds a damn thing wrong with her. He is such a mama's boy. I want to strike out at her. Strike out at their special relationship. Why do I want to hurt him so much? Maybe this is all projection and I am really talking about myself. Am I the man in my marriage? Am I the ultimate provider, protector and punisher?

I hand George the soap and cloth to scrub my back. He joins me in the shower and starts washing me. George lathers my skin as he speaks.

"So you want to put me on the couch now? You have me fall in love with you, fuck your brains out and then you start fucking with me. And you call me a motherfucker? Do you think I am fucking you because I really want to fuck my mother? Is that what you are telling me, Martha?"

George is mediocre in his attempt to explain himself. And now I feel out of control. I turn and take the soap from him.

"Hahahaha, I always thought you wanted to fuck your father," I say just to confuse him.

We change positions and George gets under the water.

"Oh, I give up, Martha. Why don't you run for president? Oh, you can't. You're a convicted felon. I can't even get your vote," George says vindictively.

He turns around and I start washing his back and shoulders.

"Don't even try to be competitive with me. You aren't smart enough. You're a stupid little Bush. You were named after a vagina. Sissy little pussy Bush."

I finish lathering his back and put him under the shower to rinse off.

"Stop it, Martha." He sounds pitiful. From my perch, I start to pity him but I'm also getting hot. I think he is, too. I start slowly washing between my legs, my labia, foaming my pussy folds.

"Poor George. Should have been a gynecologist with a name like that. He was only good at looking at pussy. But George couldn't have gotten into medical school if he tried. 'Cause he's a stupid little Bush. A humiliated Bush. A stupid Bush with attention deficit. Can't hold a thought. Can't come up with anything on his own. No ideas."

I say this slowly, with my fingers on my clit.

I take my hand out of my snatch and bring it over to his hard cock. I grab his cock and give it a little pull and hold it tight.

"Please, Martha, stop. Please. Stop. Please stop. Please."

For a moment I act like the kidding has stopped. I kiss his ear and nibble his lobe and whisper in his ear.

"A Junior Mint Bush."

George is holding his ears.

"Don't call me Junior."

I am laughing at him, "Can I call you…mama's boy?"

I turn off the water, thrust open the curtain leaving George alone in the tub, and gather one of my lavender Martha towels. I dry myself and wrap a towel around my body.

For a moment I think I should let him go down on me. My puss is in agony. I'm throbbing, pulsating. I want to fuck hard. But I have to do everything in this relationship. Even the fucking. I'm over it. Everything seems comical all of a sudden. Everything seems surreal.

"Who's the real George? George Washington? Then I am Martha Washington. I am the first lady after all, George. George and Martha Washington. George and Martha. Hahahaha. Like in 'Who's Afraid of Virginia Woolf' You probably don't even know who Edward Albee is!"

I turn on the blow dryer and tousle my hair with a little product.

George is relieved the subject is changing. "Wasn't he in 'Green Acres'? I loved that show."

George gets out of the shower. His mood is happier. He uses the towel I dropped on the floor.

"George, that's Eddie Albert, not Edward Albee. I can't believe that you don't know one of the most influential twentieth-century American playwrights. Didn't you at least see the movie?"

"If it was in black and white the answer is no." George uses my toothbrush.

"How can someone so stupid be in control of the most powerful country in the world?"

I look at George over the sink.

"Come on, George, give me the stupid look. You look so cute when you look so stupid."

George rinses his mouth. He seems defeated, but also like he doesn't care. Which makes me meaner and madder.

"I wish I was smarter for you, Martha."

I turn off the hair dryer.

"George, you must have some redeeming qualities? What are they again?"

I brush my teeth.

"I wish I could have more courage, more strength, more intelligence."

From the side of my mouth while brushing, I tell him, "The whole world is laughing at George."

"Laughing at me?" He rolls on antiperspirant. I rinse.

"Don't you get it? You're the man with the weapons of mass destruction. You are the one who is out of control. You are the evildoer.

Haven't you ever heard of projection?"

I know I'm right. And I'm not turned on anymore.

"Do you have to ruin my weekend? You always have to ruin our weekends, Martha. Whenever we have any time together, this always happens."

George gets a drink. I put on some raisin lip-gloss and apply eye crème. I'm annoyed with him, and I'm not going to let that go.

"Don't you understand anything about psychology? Saddam is your shadow. You're the man in the hole. You are Saddam Hussein. You are always saying that Saddam wanted to kill your father. The reality is that you feel so guilty about your own feelings of patricide, you disguise the taboo through your desire to capture and destroy Saddam."

Shit, I'm better than Doctor Phil.

"You really know how to hurt a guy. There goes my hard-on."
"Yes, George, you just said it. Your father makes you impotent."

"Don't turn my words around. I'm fucked up, but I love my parents." George is still in the bathroom putting some gel in his hair. He looks in the mirror. He needs a shave. He takes out the razor.

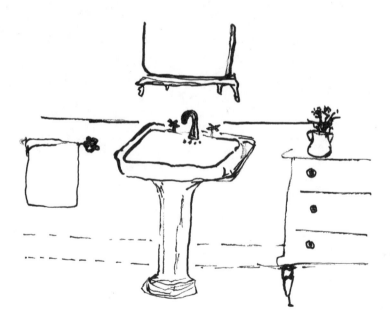

"Martha, I haven't done anything wrong. I am just trying to bring the democratic process to the Arab world."

"And the Iraqis will say, 'I lost my entire family during American bombings, but I will be able to cast a vote. Thank you, America!' Now that's freedom." I sneer sarcastically.

George comes out of the bathroom and stands over me on the bed.

"That's right. This is about morality. It is about punishing insurgents and their impulses to kill. I know there are good Iraqis. I feel for the mothers of Iraq. Many of the children no longer have fathers. And the mothers have to provide. But the oil will flow. Oil is what makes America run. It is what our economy is based on. And Iraq has to understand their place in the world, even if it means being destroyed in the process. My father didn't understand this. I wish he did. Then I wouldn't have to be taking care of this."

"Have you ever thought, George, that your intense yearnings and passionate feelings for Iraq are perverse? That it's sexual tension, George?"

I am starting to get hungry. I guess we could order in. Maybe I'll get a BLT.

"This isn't spin the bottle, Martha. I want the best for Iraq. I love Iraq."

"That's right, George. Iraq is the love of your life. Iraq is your girlfriend. Iraq is your bitch. Iraq is your whore. Iraq is your cunt. Iraq is your love object. And you have fucked her good."

"I am going to pretend I didn't hear that, Martha."

"George, Iraq is the mother that you control and destroy. You greedily devour her milk, her oil, and you kill all of her children. You occupy and invade your mother. Your preoccupation with Iraq is maternal stalking madness."

"What do you want to hear, Martha? What do you want from me? What do you want me to confess to?" He is shrieking.

I need to eat something. My blood sugar is falling. I pick up the phone and order sandwiches from the deli.

George tries to show remorse for his past.

"Okay, I slipped. So I shouldn't have stopped going to meetings." George was making sense, trying to calm things down between us. But it's no use. I am on a rampage.

I pretend I am drunk with a Texas accent: "I know it is our fault, the country's fault, for giving me the money. I don't know what happened to the money. I had money when I came into office and before you know it $300 billion is gone and hey, what's a trillion? Who's counting when you are having fun? We are a rich country, we'll get it back. One day at a time, with the help of the higher power."

 There's nothing like a dry drunk. I pour myself another drink. George is already finishing a beer.

"I didn't spend anything we didn't have, Martha. I mean, it's only money…and a few lives. But I know you only care about the money. Maybe if you weren't so concerned about your company you could have concentrated more on me and I wouldn't have been so lonely. I wouldn't have been so desperate. This is really all of your fault, Martha. It's all your fault. You weren't there for me. You were only concerned about your profits, your company, you you you. You really know how to ruin my weekend. You always have to bring politics into everything. You think too much, Martha. Maybe if you loved me for who I am I wouldn't need to act out. Martha, all I need is to be loved."

 I turn my back on the idiot and watch the twins at the convention on the TV. I wonder if George and I had had daughters, what they would look like. For a second I consider that maybe my eggs were taken out of me and inserted into Laura…But that's crazy. I have to get off the sauce.

"Do I have to love your death instinct?" I ask.

George comes over to the bar. God, he is drunk. I look back at the TV. I feel sorry for Laura. She doesn't even know how to pick out a dress. But then there's me. I suddenly feel lost and empty.

"Yes, I like to keep the nation at the pulse of a trigger. When someone is holding a gun to your head and the trigger is about to be pulled, you don't know if you're going to be alive or thrown into chaos. I'm not fighting the war, the war is fighting me," argues George.

I want to shake him out of his insanity.

"Stop playing those mind-fucking games like my father!" I shout. I'm confused. Oh, I wish this would all stop. I wish we could start the weekend over and just love each other.

"I I I love you, George, but I hate the way you make me feel."

My voice is sounding shrill, which I despise.

"I don't know why I always come back for more. I just get so desperate. You have the twins. You have that doting wife. All I have is a refrigerator to fill."

I try to be affectionate.

Please show me affection.

Suddenly, I need his love, his understanding.

I continue: "So I have abandonment issues, separation anxiety. Everyone has something. But I stay with you, George. Maybe it's better to feel abuse than to feel nothing at all."

I look up at George, my lover, and speak from my heart for the first time all night: "I am afraid of being loved so I love being hated. I'm afraid of being wanted so I want to be abused. I am afraid of being alone so I alone become afraid. I am afraid of being successful so I successfully become nothing.

"All I want is to create the fantasy that maybe we can live in a more beautiful place even when evil lurks in the hearts of men."

I look down after my speech and George very gently holds my wrists and brings my hands to his lips. He kisses my palms and then holds them tightly together as if my hands were his hands.

"Bravo, Martha. Did you write that yourself? Martha, you are the one in control. Martha, how can I be in control if you are? Martha always knows what's right. Martha knows best. Martha the know-it-all. Martha never makes a mistake. Do you, Martha? Do you feel better, Martha? Thank you, Martha, for putting me in contact with my stupidity.

But Martha, you need stupid, inept subhumans like me to maintain your sense of entitlement and grandiosity. Because actually, Martha, you don't feel worthy. Martha, you are the one out of control with your anxiety. Yes, Martha, I feel so out of control. Martha, I want to destroy the world. Destroy America. Destroy our economy. Destroy young happy Americans with a future. Destroy culture. I enjoy seeing youth die. Not because of oil, Martha. But because, Martha, I am evil. I am evil. I am the evildoer. Martha, I am in control. This time the stupid idiot calls the shots."

I spit in his face. The sandwiches should be here by now.

LOVE HURTS

Later the same day George and I are sleeping peacefully when suddenly, without warning, George bolts up in a panic.

At first I think he was having a nightmare, screaming and kicking. I can barely see him in the dark.

"AHAHAHAHAHA!!!!" George screams.

I am jolted by his distress. I try to orient myself.
"What is it, George?"

I turn on the bed light and I see George is as white as sin itself. He is having a hard time talking, he is so frantic. I hope he isn't going to throw up. I hate the mess.

"George, what is it?"

George is crawling around the bed on all fours. He is a caged, rabid animal. It's like his skin is turned inside out.

It's always something with George.

I want to go back to sleep. I want a romantic, sexy weekend. For a moment I envy Monica Lewinsky. Yeah, give me the cigar and the dress. You bet I'm a friend of Bill's.

But then George snaps me out of my petty identification with Monica.

He reveals his news.

"Bin Laden is in me! Bin Laden is hiding in me! I swallowed bin Laden," shrieks George.

George isn't just hysterical, he's foaming at the mouth. I feel like throwing a fizzy into his trap, locking the door on his hallucination and dropping him off at the rubber room at Bellevue.

Please God, what should I do with this lunatic?

As usual, Mommy takes over.

"George, settle down. You are just having a crack attack."

Maybe I should call Barbara, I think to myself. How do I deal with a situation like this? Should I check my speed dial? Believe the bastard? Go along with him? Now that's an angle.

"He's in you, George?" I ask with genuine concern.

"Yes, bin Laden is in me, Martha. You got to get him out. He's hiding in me."

We are both on the bed. George is on his knees crying for help.

"I need an exorcist. Get me the Vatican! Get me Barbara Walters! Get me 'Trading Spaces.' Get me 'Queer Eye for the Straight Guy.' Get me Craig's List! Get me out of me!"

George has his finger down his throat and is trying to throw up. I am prepared to call man overboard.

"Let me have a look, George." I grab my handy flashlight that I keep on the edge of the bed and get on my knees and peer into George's throat. George sticks out his tongue and opens wide.

"Do you see him?" asks George, as if I would keep the information to myself.

"I don't know if that is a tonsil or a terrorist." I decide to go along with the hysteria. (I'm glad he can't get a third term.)

"You can't tell the difference?"

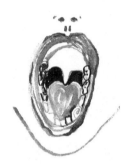

I'm straining to look past the gold bridgework. But I don't see bin Laden.

"Are you sure he came in this way, George? He could have come in the back end."

George sits on his haunches and gives it a thought.

"You've got a point, Martha. I thought that was your finger I felt…"

George gets on all fours and moves his bottom up into my face. What an asshole!

"It will be more than a finger, George…when Homeland Security comes in…"

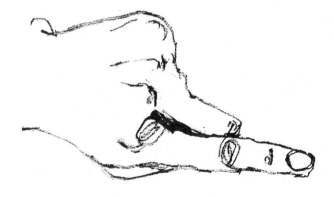

"Homeland Security, *Home Alone*, "Home Improvement." Drop the Tim Allen and look up my ass," commands our Commander-in-Chief.

I adjust my flashlight. George pulls his cheeks apart.

"George, I think I see him. George, he's in there. He's waving. He's in the canyon, the mountains," I gasp.

"Yes, there he is. Oh, for God's sake, for Allah's sake, there is bin Laden. And he's tall, too." George stays on all fours.

"Yeah, he's fucking with me, Martha. Either I am going to have to shit him out or take it up the ass."

Don't give up now, George.

"George, I wonder what would work better, a coffee or wheat grass enema?" It's the best I can offer.

George peers over at me.

"Martha, why don't you stop using my colon for comparison shopping? The problem with you liberal types is that I have bin Laden up my ass and you're asking why. Honey, my ass is Central Intelligence so let's keep the whys out of it."

Oh, the familiar George is back. I am relieved.

His tone is starting to normalize. The panic is subsiding.

"If only we could trade places and I could go to prison like you… You know what happens in prison," reasons George.

I sit back and wonder for the last time, What is in this for me? When I realize there is nothing, my sarcasm returns.

"George, maybe you have something here. This is a great photo

op. Let's put a hood on you and leash you up. Grab your nuts, put the dogs on you and I have my November cover for *Living*."

"Do you have to turn our personal life into a media opportunity? Living in a president's asshole?"

George mopes. "I wish I could take your place. If only I was going to prison like you."

He's rubbing a little too hard with the wipe. I might have to take it away from him. What a baby.

"You aren't going to absolve yourself through my jail sentence."

It's time to start packing my things before another America's Most Wanted shows up intravenously. There is only so much I can take.

"It sounds like a vacation if you ask me," George says with a sneer.

"A vacation?"

I know the insults will be next.

"You are always so fucking busy with tedious, unimportant, meaningless tasks. You are so anal, Martha."

I knew it. George sees me packing and he is mad at me for leaving.

"George, don't get angry with me because bin Laden is making you use your sphincter."

"You drive me crazy, Martha. Your mad need for order, order

and more order. There is nothing sexy about you, Martha, except maybe your attention to detail."

"George, don't even try to figure me out. Let's not ruin a good thing. I have my own way of doing things. It helps, George. Every minor detail takes on a life of its own. The closet is my executioner. I move towards the closet, or a pantry, as if it is a guillotine. I open a door in dread, searching through hangers, sorting through drawers…"

The room becomes cold. The mood changes. I'm leaving. Mommy is leaving.

George is making the separation easier by making it difficult. George is going insane, not making sense. He is a child. I will have to spell everything out for him.

"Don't start now, George. Let's not ruin a good thing. Let me leave now and go to prison. And I will see you when both of us are out of a job."

"Martha, you are talking to the guy who was designated by God to be in a special place of power. So let me play God, not you. You aren't leaving me. God doesn't want you to leave me. If you leave me, I will die, Martha. I am nothing without you."

I put on a zebra wrap-around skirt, but the belt is too long. Poor design.

"God? Can we keep God out of our relationship? Can we set a God boundary? God doesn't want me to go? All I remember is you played God when you wanted me to have an abortion." Now I said it. Now I finally told our truth. I expect George to have feelings of regret. Instead…

"Martha, I wanted you to have an abortion because I didn't want a devil giving birth. You would suffocate our baby with all of your… I am

88

sorry Martha... I shouldn't have said that our baby died," laments George, abruptly changing his tone.

I stop my packing. He has crossed a line. He has to hurt me.

George is like every other man. If he hurts then everyone will hurt.

Here I am going off to prison and he says everything and anything to hurt me. My heart is in my belly. I want to be with my daughter. At least I have her.

I decide to be a better mother. A better person for her and for me. All of a sudden I realize I've been living for everyone else and not for me.

"I should have called my magazine *Dying. Martha Stewart Dying.* All of my hard work, all of my efforts, all of my energy is to keep from dying. My emptiness creeps up on me and I do more and more: iron a shirt, prune the roses, can the tomatoes. I could be pulling the trigger, but instead I'm pulling the weeds. I could be slicing my wrists, but I am slicing the beefsteak tomatoes. I could be hanging myself, but I am hanging the sheets out to dry in the sun. I could be putting a hole in my heart, a hole in my head, a hole in my soul, but instead I am putting a hole in my plaster wall.

"These are my rituals, my own dealmakers to stop myself from dying. In doing I lose all sense of myself. I have become Martha the Machine. Martha Non-human. Martha Not-Living."

I feel so low. My life feels like nothing. I have nothing left.

George starts to get dressed too. He pulls on his dress slacks and a blue shirt.

"Martha, you know this whole case of insider trading is a set-up. We want you to join the CIA, give you a cover and work on a special project. That's why you are going to jail. You are working for us now."

"No, George. I am not going to work for you. For years I protected myself from the feelings I never dared express. No one can make Martha suffer. Martha can endure any pain. No one can hurt Martha because no amount of pain can equal Papa's hurting me." I cry.

George is watching me pack. I am putting all of my accessories away.

"Okay, Martha, trump me on the bad childhood but look, I'm a puppet president. It was either this or becoming the biggest coke dealer in Texas.

"Baby, you aren't going to jail. Look, baby, I love you. And that's that."

George looks at me like I am his daughter, and for a moment I want to weep. For a second I want to be saved. I want to be rescued. But it would only be temporary. It would only be in George's best interest.

"But I want to go to jail. I need

somewhere to go. I need to be looked after and cared for. I need a father's protection. I need to be punished and taken care of. That's why I need jail. Don't tell me what I need. Don't make my decisions for me."

George turns away and mixes a drink.

"You're not leaving me, Martha, and that's that. Now it is all set up. You don't have to go to jail. Why do you insist on the drama?"

George certainly could be competent when the need arose. But I always resist his daddy act.

"Papa never recognized my suffering. He said things like, 'You have no idea what suffering is.' Now maybe in prison I will finally be able to suffer in peace. I always thought that to suffer you had to be really special. I worked hard at being special. But I was never special enough. Maybe now I am special enough to suffer."

I zipper up my overnight bag. I think I'll throw this one out. This is the last time I will look at this luggage.

I wonder if Bloomingdale's is still open…

Maybe I should design a line of luggage.

Stop it, Martha! I always detach from the present.

"Do you really think you did anything wrong? Martha, get real.

None of the players are who they say they are. Noriega. Saddam Hussein. Shah of Iran. It was all part of a deal. That video with Saddam in the hole—you think that is real? This government is a fantasy, just like your linen closet. But then, you wouldn't understand. You are only a caterer, Martha."

Didn't I tell you? The moment I have my bags packed and zipped, he deals the final blow and ruins our time together for good.

"I'm only a caterer? What? I could give you my childhood on a celery stick, my family background on a welcome mat, my college years

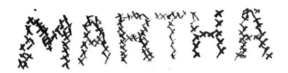

in a sachet, my Martha Stewart Living cross-stitched, my domineering personality neatly ironed and heavily starched, my public image in foie gras, my bank account in onion skin, my frenzied schedule in India ink, my tortured, calloused, bruised, tethered, scrubbed hands of a Polish peasant woman, my prom dress of handmade calico rags, my hysterectomy… Because if I was a man I could have done a better job than you!" I say with the air of a CEO.

"Yes, any one could have done a better job. But then again, I wouldn't call what you do a job."
George puts me down to the core.

"It's not a job? My job is as live-in domestic for the nation. It's slicing and dicing. It's baking basting beating brewing broiling canning chopping digging drying filleting folding freezing frying grating grilling icing making mashing mopping nesting peeling poaching pouring pruning

I know

tarragon

pureeing roasting sautéing scrubbing sewing shopping sorting steaming stewing stirring tiling toasting washing whipping.

"I know apples. Rome beauties, Empires, McIntosh and Gaia organic. I know brunch, breakfast. I know candles, glazed carrots. I know dessert. I know eggs, omelets, hollandaise, Florentine. I know gingerbread houses. I have New Hampshire in one hand and Ireland in the other. I know jams and jellies. I know kettles. I know lemon zest. I know marjoram, mopping and moisture. I know the blue of robin's eggs in nests, I have owls and ovens. I know poaching. I know potting. I know quilts. I know risotto. I know thyme, tarragon and tasting. U You You You Victory vases Y Why? Why? Because it all adds up to a big fat zero."

I pause and catch my breath.

"I am the nation's mother and everyone hates their mother."

I am crying. My heart is on fire and my passion has burned out.

"Don't take it so personally, Martha."

"George, the only thing you have personally accomplished is failure."

I pick up my suitcase and turn towards the door.

"Oh, go on, Martha, why stop now. Continue with Life According to Martha."

I need to break free, but George stops me. He holds me. I can't get away. I am getting claustrophobic. I need air. I need freedom.

"Why don't you do something that is more in tune with your abilities? Why don't you do something about parking?" I snarl, looking straight into his eyes. Suddenly I feel like I am standing up to every man who has taken advantage of me for being female.

"How horrible are you, Martha? How hateful is Martha?"

I wonder if he is talking to me or to himself.

"You hate Martha. I hate Martha! Everyone hates Martha!" I shout.

I am defending myself. I am trying to break loose. I am clobbering George with the suitcases. Look at me! I have always been so good. I was the good girl. The good daughter. The good wife. The good student. The good mother. The good neighbor. The good employer. But I guess I was never good enough.

"I hate you, George. I hate you. I hate everything about you. Do you know what I love most about you, George? Hating you. I love to hate you."

I calm down or maybe I give up. Does it matter?

George's expression changes. "It's moments like this that I realize I can't live without you, when you are more incoherent than me... Don't leave me, Martha. You can't leave me. Not now. I love Martha. Not the do-it-all Martha, but the vulnerable Martha. You can do so much, I know. But I can make you smile, take your mind off things, make you laugh. You're my little girl. See, all I got from my parents was, 'Not in this family, George. That's enough, son.'"

In the final analysis, George always has to make it about him. He is such a narcissist, and I am merely an extension of him. He'd never understand me. Why have I spent so many years expecting him to?

"George, I didn't have the goddamn privileges that you were born into. You were expected to rule the world whether you couldn't, shouldn't or wouldn't. I was not expected to be talented. My reality is every woman's reality. I am being abandoned by society for refusing to be the weaker sex, refusing to be passive, refusing to be as cute as possible, to be as desirable as possible, as boring as possible. Yes, Mr. President, I took the unpaid housewife and gave her a fair deal, I gave her life meaning. I gave her value. My crime is that I am not sorry. I am not sorry. So, lock me up!"

I look straight at him with the strength of a mother who can pick up a car if her child is underneath. I have adrenaline rushing through my veins. I feel the years of work of all women. I feel the tireless, thankless work of women as nurse, cook and maid.

"I have always thought of you as a domestic terrorist, Martha. Your own hyper domestic designer version of terror, of a controlled lifestyle of abuse. Don't worry, Martha. We have a special relationship. You won't be going to prison."

I put on my gray, sequined, crocheted shawl over my shoulders, slip my white, patent leather sling backs on my feet, and place my hand firmly on the doorknob.

"George, I am always told to remember those less fortunate than myself. To remember the homeless, the poor, the suffering. Well, I am suffering inside! Any time I see anyone caring, sharing loving, I break down inside with envy. That's why I want to be locked up, because I will feel comfortable surrounded by the less fortunate, the broken, the collapsed, the guilty... Because it looks like how I feel inside. It looks like what I feel like inside. So don't take that away from me, the

one thing I earned on my own…my own punishment on my own terms. I want to feel. I am no longer going to feel the only feeling of no feelings at all."

Tears are running down my face. I feel so lonely. I know I won't be missed for being me, but for what I can do for others, for George.

I am so distraught, I don't realize how drunk George is. I should order him a double espresso. Look at me, I just can't stop thinking about others' needs…

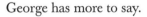

George has more to say.

"Yeah, I'm lucky. I'm so so lucky. I hate people. I hate people who rationalize luck. I hate people who have to have a reason for everything. They just can't accept evil. They just can't accept that good things happen to bad people. Or that bad people have good luck. I admit it. I am out of control I am out of control. I am out of control!"

George becomes a stranger, so distant to me, right then and there.

I turn the doorknob and start to walk out the door.

"Martha? Martha! Don't leave me. You're not going anywhere. I need you, Martha. Martha! Baby. Baby. Baby." His voice is part of my past now.

I stand by the door as it closes. I think he will run after me. But I guess that is my vanity. I need to stop being needed. Oh, this hurts too much.

From the closed door, I can hear George is doing just fine. He

tie a yellow ribbon
around an old oak tree

is talking to himself. He is probably finishing up the coke, checking the convention on the TV.

I stand alone in the hallway and listen.

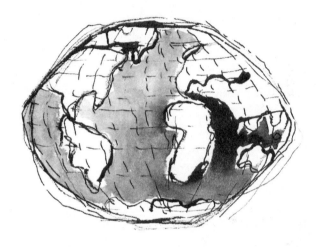

"I hate independence. Independence Day. I don't need to be dependent on Martha. Hahaha. I want Dependence Day. I want to be dependent on drugs, alcohol, sex and a woman I don't love. I want dependency. I am taking away all the independence of this country. I will take away abortion, I will take away freedom of speech. In George's world no one can talk because everyone becomes a baby. Baby Nation. This stupid flag–wave it wave it, Daddy! Wave the flag. Wave the diaper. We're all in Depends in this country. Yeah, I care more about the flag than I do about my own citizens' hungry bellies. I care more about a goddamn yellow ribbon, like it's your binky, your pacifier, than I do about people dying in Iraq. Homeland security, what a crock… Let me tell you, God has failed. God is bureaucracy. God is statistics. God is the price of oil based on the euro not the dollar. God is my father when you don't have a father who loves you, who wants you, who believes in you. God is what you make and not what you feel. So you see, Martha, I am a very, very religious man. I live in a state of never getting better. I live in a world of caving in. I live a life where pleasure means death. It's a life of lies, Martha. It's a life of selling out. I'm a living hell and I intend to keep my devil out."

I walk past the rooms ready to be made up. In the distance I hear lovers making love on squeaky beds, or tricks turned for pennies. Two runaways share their dreams, a single mother awaits her welfare, a mental patient tries not to take his own life.

A maid for the hotel passes me by with clean sheets. She speaks in Polish.

I understand. She says, "This is life."

You need to be lost in order to find your way.

Acknowledgments

This book started as a play. Initially I was planning on writing "Bush: The Musical," but while I was backstage at the Illusion Theatre in Minneapolis, the concept of "George & Martha" took hold. "George & Martha" premiered at The Collective Unconscious in Manhattan in September 2004. It was a co-production with PS122. Neal Medlyn played George and I played Martha.

I would like to thank the following people: Amy Scholder, Rex Ray, Giles O'Bryen, Gavin Browning, Rachel Guidera, and the staff at Verso. Michael Robbins, David Leslie, Neal Medlyn, Ron Lasko, Caterina Bartha, Don Guarnieri, Scott Griffin, Will Magnum, Gary Hayes, Becky Hubbert, Chris Tanner, Stephen Hammel, Steven Menendez, Brandon Olson, Nancy Gray, Nan Becker, Michael Overn, the entire staff of PS122, the entire staff of The Collective Unconscious, Barbet Schroeder, Timothy and Karin Greenfield-Sanders, Randy Martin, Anita Dwyer, and the Art and Public Policy faculty, staff and students. I am indebted to all my siblings—Carol, John, James, Will and Brian. And of course my gratitude to my precious daughter Violet.

This book is dedicated to the memory of Finley Peter Dunne.

Photo: Timothy Greenfield-Sanders

Karen Finley is a New York-based artist whose transgressive performances have long provoked controversy and debate. She has exhibited her visual art and performed her plays internationally. She is the author of *Shock Treatment, Enough Is Enough, Living It Up, Pooh Unplugged* and *A Different Kind of Intimacy*, and the editor of *Aroused: A Collection of Erotic Writings*. She is currently a professor in Art and Public Policy at Tisch School of the Arts, New York University.

father of our country

Larry King listens to Karen Hughes

WITHDRAWAL

St. Martha
patron saint of